To Mungo Taylor who would never be naughty like Mr. Davies

First U.S. edition 1996

Library of Congress Cataloging-in-Publication Data

Voake, Charlotte.
Mr. Davies and the baby / Charlotte Voake. — 1st U.S. ed.
Summary: A mother and baby greatly miss Mr. Davies, the dog, when
his owner ties him up so he can't cause trouble while walking with them,
but Mother finds another solution.
ISBN 1-56402-390-7
[1. Dogs—Fiction. 2. Babies—Fiction. 3. Walking—Fiction.] I. Title.
PZ7.V855Mp   1996
[E]—dc20   95-11338

10 9 8 7 6 5 4 3 2 1

Printed in Hong Kong

This book was handlettered by Charlotte Voake.
The pictures were done in watercolor and ink.

Candlewick Press
2067 Massachusetts Avenue
Cambridge, Massachusetts 02140

Mr. Davies
and the Baby

Charlotte
Voake

CANDLEWICK PRESS
CAMBRIDGE, MASSACHUSETTS

ONCE upon a time there was a little dog named Mr. Davies. All day long he stayed in his yard.

He sniffed the smells and dug holes in the flower beds.

He ate his meals,
and when it rained, he

slept in his doghouse.

Next door to Mr. Davies

lived a baby.

Every single day the baby and his mother went out for a walk.

"Hello, Mr. Davies," the baby's mother said. The baby clapped his hands and laughed, and Mr. Davies wagged his tail. Mr. Davies watched them go down the road and wished he could go with them.

Then one day
Mr. Davies found he
could squeeze
right under
the gate,
and he
came out
to meet
the baby.

The baby was very excited.
So was Mr. Davies, and
he jumped
around and
wagged his
tail.
"Nice dog,"
said the
baby's mother.
"Now, go home, Mr. Davies."

But Mr. Davies was much
too excited to listen.
He just wagged his
tail harder
and followed
them down
the road.

Mr. Davies was very good until he saw some ducks.

"Mr. Davies, come here!" shouted the baby's mother.

The next day,
Mr. Davies went
for a walk
with the
baby
again.
But this
time he
chased
a cat.

WOOF!

And the next day, Mr. Davies saw a man on a bicycle and chased him up the road.

People asked the baby's mother, "Is this your dog?" "No, he is not," she said.

One day the baby's mother
went next door.

"Please, could you keep
Mr. Davies from getting out
of the yard?" she asked.

The next day, Mr. Davies ran
to meet the baby

and the baby held out
his arms.

But just as Mr. Davies got to the gate, he came to a sudden STOP.

Poor Mr. Davies had been tied to his doghouse!

He barked
and barked

but he could not get free.

The baby and his mother set off down the road. Soon they couldn't hear Mr. Davies barking anymore. The baby was sad. Even the baby's mother was sorry that Mr. Davies had been tied up.

It was very quiet.

Then suddenly they heard a SMASHING and a BANGING and a happy BARKING coming toward them.

It was Mr. Davies...

and he was bringing

his doghouse with him!

The very next day, the baby and his mother bought Mr. Davies a beautiful leash.

Now he goes walking
with them every day,
and everyone is happy,

even the
ducks!